Horace looked at his flock. He had never seen such a healthy bunch of canaries. They were fit, strong and ready for anything – which was just as well, because for what Horace had in mind they would need to be. But were they strong enough? He considered for a moment, then made up his mind.

'If we're not ready now,' he said to himself, 'we never will be!'

When Horace gave the word to begin, the canaries let out a great cheer and sprang into position.

'Ready!' they cried in muffled voices.

'On the count of three!' shouted Horace. 'One, two, THREE!'

The six canaries pulled with all their might, tugging the two bars away from each other. All those beak and neck exercises were being put to good use.

Slowly, the bars began to bend apart . . .

The Keep-Fit Canaries

Jonathan Allen

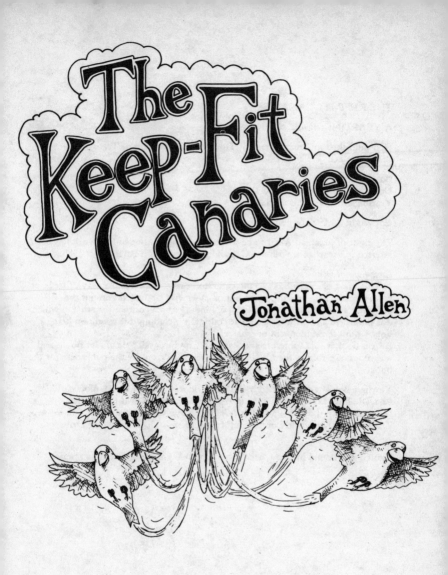

YEARLING BOOKS

THE KEEP-FIT CANARIES

A YEARLING BOOK 0 440 86293 0

First published in Great Britain by Doubleday, a division of Transworld Publishers Ltd

PRINTING HISTORY
Doubleday edition published 1992
Yearling edition published 1993

Yearling Books are published by Transworld Publishers Ltd, 61–63 Uxbridge Road, Ealing, London W5 5SA, in Australia by Transworld Publishers (Australia) Pty. Ltd, 15–25 Helles Avenue, Moorebank, NSW 2170, and in New Zealand by Transworld Publishers (N.Z.) Ltd, 3 William Pickering Drive, Albany, Auckland.

Printed and bound in Great Britain by Cox & Wyman Ltd, Reading, Berks.

CHAPTER 1
SWEET LITTLE BIRDIES

The seven canaries sat in their cage in the pet shop window, looking bored. Sometimes people stopped and looked in at them, but mostly they preferred instead to watch the puppies, kittens, cockatiels, rabbits and other unfortunate creatures that shared the canaries' window-space.

Horace, the canaries' leader, wiled away the time by playing 'Spot the Canary Fancier' which, although it wasn't very exciting, beat playing with bits of cuttlefish, plastic pretend budgies, and those small round jingling things with mirrors on.

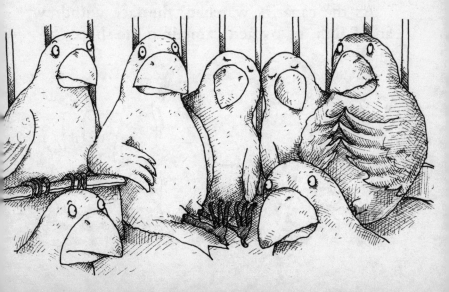

'Canary Fanciers' were people who tapped on the glass and made muffled whistling and trilling noises, trying to attract the birds' attention.

'Hello,' said Horace, giving Boris, his second in command, a nudge. 'This looks like one.'

He nodded to a face that was pressed against the window. It had a big, soppy smile spread across it.

'You could be right,' said Boris. 'Look at that grin! Oh dear, oh dear, a sad case!' He shook his head.

'I bet you anything he starts making stupid whistling noises and waving,' said Horace. 'I'll give him five seconds. Five – four – three – two — Yes! There he goes, waving like a maniac! Now that's what I call a Canary Fancier!'

As the canaries watched, the face withdrew and Ralph, its owner, came into the shop.

'How much are those charming canaries in the window?' he asked.

The pet shop owner smiled broadly. 'I can do you a special deal on them,' he said. 'Cage included!'

The canaries grinned and nudged each other as Ralph, their new owner, carried their cage out of the shop. As Ralph left, Mr Pettigrew, the pet shop man, gave him a useful tip.

'Keep their cage in the window,' he said, 'and the little darlings will sing fit to burst!'

This was just what Ralph wanted.

'The happy sound of birdsong!' he sighed. 'I shall fill my humble home with delightful sounds!'

He was looking forward to getting home and, as the bus bumped along, he day-dreamed contentedly about the wonderful, canary-filled life ahead of him. He imagined being woken by gentle twittering as the morning sun streamed in through the window.

He imagined being greeted in the evening by a glorious chorus of welcome, his little feathery friends singing their hearts out, so pleased that he, their beloved owner, had come home to them. Ralph smiled to himself as he pictured the happy scene.

★

But needless to say, what Ralph wanted wasn't what he got. His dream of cheerfully chirping canaries hopping happily around in their cage was not to be. The canaries had other ideas.

In the morning, as the sunlight streamed into the room, they didn't sing. Instead they put dark glasses on and slouched around their food tray in tight-beaked silence. And when Ralph called 'Sing little birdies!' they just looked at him. One of them even belched. That was disappointing, but it was the seed-spitting that really got him down.

Ralph would spend his evenings hunched miserably in front of the television, seeds bouncing off his forehead, ears and nose, picking the bigger ones out of his sausage sandwich. It was depressing – the canaries just didn't act the way they were supposed to.

CHAPTER 2

WHAT'S YELLOW AND ANTISOCIAL?

Ralph just couldn't work it out. He racked his brains to try and find a reason for the canaries' behaviour. Perhaps they have a grudge against people generally, he thought. It would explain why they didn't seem to like him all that much. Maybe the poor things had been mistreated in the past. I must try to be more understanding.

He pictured himself gently tending his poor, misunderstood canaries, nobly turning the other cheek to their seed-spitting, all the while smiling a smile that said, 'I understand!'

A sunflower seed in the eye brought him back down to earth. He jumped to his feet.

'You little . . .!' he began, but stopped himself just in time. 'Little dears!' he said finally, and smiled an understanding smile.

Ralph's reaction confused the canaries. Boris watched and wondered.

'Do you think it's working?' he whispered to Horace.

'Not like it ought to,' replied Horace. 'I'm worried. He's not responding at all. And *urgh*! As for that cheesy grin he's started pulling, what's all that about?'

'I dunno. Maybe he's trying to make us sick,' said Boris. 'It bothers me the way he just sits there, letting it all happen. 'What's wrong with him?'

'It's what's wrong with our planning that worries me,' muttered Horace, shaking his head.

He watched the seeds bouncing off Ralph's unresponsive head and sighed.

'It's not like our last owner – you remember, Old Fish Face. The one who lived in the basement flat with the tacky wallpaper.'

10

'Old Fish Face' was the canaries' nickname for a quiet, sensitive, retired music teacher called Mr Mathews. He had bought the canaries to keep him company, and to delight him with their sweet, melodious singing. Some hope! From the first they had refused to sing and instead had banged on the bars of the cage, making a distinctly unmelodious pinging noise. By taking it in turns they had managed to keep up this horrible racket right round the clock. After two days of this, Mr Mathews could stand it no more and took the canaries back to the shop. He was so upset he didn't even ask for his money back.

'I remember him!' cried Boris. 'It only took us two days to drive him half-mental. That was a good plan, that was!'

'Yes, but then what happened?' complained Horace. 'Did he let us go? No, he did not! He took us back to the shop. So did all our other owners before that. We put in all that effort, all that planning, and who's benefiting from it? The pet shop owner, that's who! Old Pettigrew! I bet he can't believe his luck! He's sold us nine times now, while here we are no nearer to freedom than before!'

'I hadn't thought of it like that,' said Boris, 'but you're right.'

'Yes,' continued Horace, 'unfortunately I am. I wish I could say that this time it's going to be different, but I get this nasty feeling that whatever we do, the best we can expect is a trip back to the pet shop. It's not good enough!'

Boris and the other canaries, who had gathered round to listen, murmured agreement. Horace was giving it to them straight.

'The only time anything different happened was when we pretended to fall down dead. Remember that? We nearly got fed to the cat! If we hadn't staged a miraculous recovery it would have been curtains. No, we need a better plan, a plan that will get us out of this cage for good!'

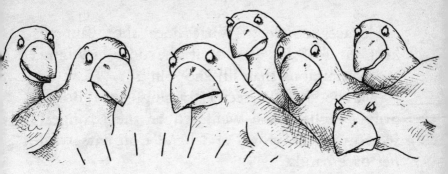

The canaries cheered half-heartedly. They were beginning to despair of finding a way of escape, and the realization that all their previous efforts had been in vain was a heavy blow.

'Come on, canaries!' cried Horace. 'Are we going to sink into gloom and despair? No!'

As Horace was speaking, the lady in the flat below Ralph's put on her keep-fit exercise record very loudly. The canaries groaned.

'How are we supposed to think with that row going on?' they muttered.

'Work those thighs!' went the record. 'One two, one two!'

Horace scowled. 'What does she want to keep fit for? It's not as if she does anything more strenuous than lift shopping.'

'Maybe she's in secret training,' said Boris, drily. 'Perhaps she wants to be the strongest woman in the world and bend iron bars with her bare hands.'

Horace's face lit up.

'Boris!' he exclaimed. 'You're a genius! That's it! Gather round canaries!' he shouted over the noise of the record. 'I've got an idea!'

CHAPTER 3

WHAT'S YELLOW AND IN THE PINK ?

In an effort to make his life a little easier, Ralph had bought a wide-brimmed hat to protect himself from the worst of the seed-spitting.

As he approached the door of his flat he took a deep breath and put the hat on, tilting the brim so that it covered as much of his face as possible. Then he opened the door and edged into the room.

He was about to make his usual dive for the safety of the chair by the television, when he stopped. Something was different. The canaries hadn't spat a single seed at him since he'd entered the room. Were they ill? Cautiously he looked round, expecting a surprise attack at any moment. No, they didn't seem to be ill. There they were in their cage, grooming their feathers and daintily eating their seed, for all the world like a bunch of ordinary songbirds. The change was remarkable. Ralph was encouraged.

'Patient loving care,' he said to himself smugly. 'It works wonders.' He laughed. 'Who knows, one day soon they might even sing for me.'

With a light heart, he sat down and tucked into his sausage sandwich, relishing every seedless minute.

There were other distinct improvements in the canaries' behaviour. When Ralph fed them later that day, they didn't stand stock still and glare at him through their dark glasses like before. Instead, they hopped around and fluttered their tiny little wings. One canary gave out a tiny 'Tweet!' Ralph was delighted and shook out some more seed. The canary chirped twice.

The more seed I leave for them, he thought, the more they'll sing.

So from then on, each morning he left an enormous pile of seed in their food tray, and in return, the canaries twittered grudgingly. It was a start.

In the days that followed, Ralph watched them getting bigger and fitter.

'All that seed!' he said to himself. 'It must be good for them. What big, strong, healthy birds they are!'

And they were. They were broad in the shoulder, sleek of feather, bright-eyed and positively radiant with health. Ralph was pleased.

'This is all due to my expert treatment,' he boasted.

He was wrong, of course. If he could have seen what went on in the canary cage when he was out at work, he would have known better. He would have discovered the real reason for their dramatic improvement and found that it had very little to do with his so-called 'expert treatment'.

For two weeks now, the canaries had been in training. Every day, all day, they were engaged in strict body-building exercises – lifting the food dish, flapping with the pole, throwing the cuttlefish and beak-wrestling, to name but a few. They only paused to sleep, and to eat staggering amounts of seed.

Under their feathers, muscles of iron and sinews of steel were forming. It was all part of Horace's inspired plan. The canaries were making themselves strong.

19

CHAPTER 4

HERE WE GO, HERE WE GO, HERE WE GO!

Horace looked at his flock. He had never seen such a healthy bunch of canaries. They were fit, strong and ready for anything – which was just as well, because for what Horace had in mind they would need to be. But were they strong enough? He considered for a moment, then made up his mind.

'If we're not ready now,' he said to himself, 'we never will be!'

When Horace gave the word to begin, the canaries let out a great cheer and sprang into position. Boris, Norris and Morris flew to the side of the cage and gripped one of the bars in their beaks. Doris, Clarice and Alice gripped the bar next to it. This was the moment all their training had been leading up to.

'Ready!' they cried, in muffled voices.

'On the count of three!' shouted Horace. 'One, two, THREE!'

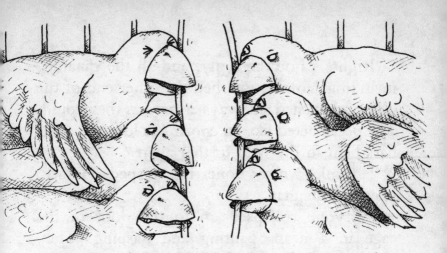

The six canaries pulled with all their might, tugging the two bars away from each other. All those beak and neck exercises were being put to good use.

Slowly, the bars began to bend apart. The canaries paused for breath, then gripped the bars once more.

'This time,' cried Horace, 'all the way!'

They strained and grunted and the bars bent still further.

'All right, stop!' he yelled, and they stopped.

While everyone was recovering their breath, Horace was busy dismantling the perch. He slid the wooden pole from the wire frame and dragged it over to the bars. Then he pushed one end into the gap.

'Ready!' he shouted, standing back.

21

'Right!' came the reply, and all the canaries, including Horace, grabbed the other end of the pole and pushed sideways as hard as they could. The perch acted like an enormous lever, and the bars bent further and further apart.

'I think we've done it!' gasped Horace, releasing his grip.

Everyone collapsed on to the floor of the cage in a heap, panting and gasping. They would have cheered if they'd had the energy.

Horace pulled the perch out of the gap and stood back. The canaries watched, holding their breath – or what there was left of it. This was an historic moment.

'A small step for canary,' said Horace solemnly, 'but a giant leap for canarykind.' Then he squeezed through the gap and out into the room.

The canaries cheered and hugged each other, not knowing whether to laugh or cry. Some of them did both. Then they too squeezed, one by one, through the gap.

'Whooeee!' yelled Doris. 'Freedom! I like it, I like it!'

'They haven't made the cage that could hold us!' shouted Morris, as he pushed through the bent bars. 'Canaries for ever!'

The canaries all cheered, and turned to help Boris out of the cage. He was the biggest and most muscular of them all, and was having a bit of trouble getting through the gap.

'Come on, you lot. Grab my wings and pull. I'm not staying here on my own!'

Norris and Morris took hold of a wing each and heaved.

'Urk!' gasped Boris. 'I'm going to be a very long and very thin canary at this rate. Ooooh! Ah! YES!'

Like a cork from a bottle, Boris shot out of the gap in the bars and cannoned into the others, knocking them flying. A laughing, flapping ball of canaries tumbled on to the table.

At that moment, Ralph came into the room.
He had taken the rest of the day off work and
come home for an early lunch.

'Oh no!' he cried, when he saw what was
happening. 'Why are you trying to escape? I
only wanted you to sing for me!'

'All right,' said Horace, 'we'll sing for you.
Come on, everybody!'

The canaries burst into song.

'Here we go, here we go, here we go!' they
sang, circling the room in tight formation. 'Here
we go, here we go, here we go-o!'

Ralph made a wild grab at them but missed. The canaries circled the room faster and faster, still singing.

'Now!' shouted Horace, and the formation changed direction and headed straight for the window. Glass is as nothing to a super-fit canary, so with seven crashes they went straight through it as though it wasn't there, leaving what looked like seven large bullet holes, and a single yellow feather swirling in their wake.

CHAPTER 5

FREE AS A BIRD, TIMES SEVEN

A large canary, travelling at high speed across the classroom, is guaranteed to grab your attention.

It certainly grabbed the attention of Mrs Thompson's English class. It was one of those hot, dreamy summer days, when everything seems to be half-asleep. The birds sang, the bees buzzed, and the teacher's voice droned on. The class was drifting into a state of hazy, vague daydreams, when, suddenly:

WHOOOOOOSH!

A huge canary zoomed in through the open window, whizzed three times round the teacher, shouted, 'Yahoo!' and zoomed out again.

The class gasped. The gasp was hardly out of their mouths when:

ZOOOOOM!

Six more large canaries whooshed into the room in tight formation, did a low, fast swoop, shouted, 'Yeehaaa!' and then split off in all directions like an Air Force display team, before zooming out again.

The class sat open-mouthed in stunned silence for a second then, with one impulse, they rushed to the window.

The canaries were falling about laughing on the school's television aerial. They slapped each other on the back and giggled uncontrollably.

'This is fun!' gasped Doris, leaning on Clarice for support while, down below, children's heads stuck out of the windows at odd angles as they tried to see where the mad canaries had gone.

'I could get to enjoy this Freedom business!' said Boris. 'That was a laugh. What shall we do next?'

Horace was in a practical mood. He felt his responsibilities as leader very keenly.

'Fun it may be,' he said, 'but there's more to life than fun. There's also food! I don't know about you lot, but I'm hungry.'

'Yeah, food!' cried Boris. 'I like the sound of that!'

'Keep talking, man, you're speaking my language,' said Doris.

28

In a quiet, leafy square a short distance away, a small man in a trilby hat was sitting on a bench eating his sandwiches. Every now and then he reached into a paper bag on his lap and threw a handful of stale crumbs to the birds that fluttered around him.

'There you are, my little dears!' he said in a kindly voice, and raised his sandwich towards his mouth for another bite. Suddenly there was a whooshing noise, a flash of yellow, and no sandwich. He stared at his empty hand in disbelief.

Up in a nearby tree, Horace and the rest of the canaries were chuckling through mouthfuls of peanut-butter sandwich.

'What's good enough for humans is good enough for us!' declared Horace, wiping his beak. 'Stale crumbs are an insult to canarykind. We will not lower ourselves by eating such rubbish!'

'Hooray!' cheered the other canaries. 'No more birdseed!'

'No more stupid bits of smelly cuttlefish,' yelled Doris, jumping up and down on her twig.

'Three cheers for Horace!'

The canaries all cheered. Then they took off, flew once in tight formation around the square and zoomed off into the sky.

CHAPTER 6

WHAT'S YELLOW AND UNBEATABLE?

'Slow down a bit, you lot!' panted Boris. 'My wings are aching something rotten.'

'Some of us haven't got so much weight to carry,' Clarice pointed out.

'Ooooh!' squealed Boris in mock horror. 'Get her! This is solid muscle, matey. Solid as rock, and then some!'

'A bit like what's inside your head then,' grinned Doris.

'Nothing wrong with a bit of heavy rock,' Boris replied. 'What do you reckon, Horace?'

'I reckon you should shut up for a minute and let me think,' said Horace.

The canaries flew on in respectful silence.

'We've had a tiring day,' Horace finally announced. 'We need to find somewhere to sleep while we've still got the energy. It's not getting any earlier.'

This sounded like good sense, so the canaries started scouting around for suitable places to rest.

'We could try under that railway bridge down there,' suggested Alice. 'It might be quite snug.'

They swooped down to have a look.

'Yuck!' said Boris when they got to the bridge. 'Dirty, dreary, damp, dingy and disgusting! And look at those tatty old specimens – I don't fancy sharing with *them*.' He waved his wing at a group of pigeons who sat hunched up on a girder.

'Charming!' said one of them. 'Ain't you got no respect? If I was a younger bird I'd come over there and peck your bottom for you!' The other pigeons muttered in agreement.

'You're not getting your crusty old beak anywhere near my bottom, sunshine!' shouted Boris. 'Urgh, what an unpleasant idea.' The canaries sniggered as they flew off.

'Why don't we try those chimney stacks over there, man?' suggested Doris. 'They might be warm and dry.'

They flew up to investigate, but the chimney stacks turned out to be cold, smelly, and full of noisy starlings.

Horace shuddered. 'I couldn't stand those twittering fidgets fluttering around all night,' he said. 'This is ridiculous. There's got to be somewhere good enough for us.'

There was, and when Horace saw it he gave a cry of delight. It was a statue of a man riding a horse and waving his sword in the air. The man wore a large, wide-brimmed hat. Horace swooped down on to it and the others followed.

'This is more like it!' said Horace. 'Make yourselves at home, folks!'

'This is our kind of style, man,' said Doris, looking round at the grand buildings in the square. 'In with the kings and princes and dukes and all them. Yeah, this is where we belong.'

'Arise, Sir Boris of the bird table!' cried Alice, tapping Boris with a long white feather she had just found. The other canaries clapped and cheered.

With much laughing and joking, the canaries sorted out who would sleep where, and were just making themselves comfortable when they were rudely interrupted.

'I hope all you pretty little yellow birdies weren't thinking of roosting here tonight,' droned a sarcastic voice, 'on account of it being *my* roosting place!'

The voice belonged to an enormous and very mean-looking seagull who stood glaring down at them from the top of the statue's hat.

Horace opened one eye. 'Are you talking to me?' he asked coldly. The seagull shrieked with mocking laughter.

'Talking to you? Of course I'm talking to you! Who do you think I'm talking to, feather face? The Queen Mother? Well, shorty, I've got a question for you. What's small and yellow with two black eyes? You don't know? Well, I'll tell you. *You* are if you don't get OFF MY ROOSTING PLACE!'

Horace glared at him.

'I think you'll find we were here first,' he said, calmly.

'Oh yeah?' squawked the seagull. 'Oh yeah? I think you'll find that I'm much, much bigger than you are, and if you little yellow seed-scrabblers don't shift your bottom feathers from my roosting place pretty fast, you're in for a serious pecking! And I'm talking SERIOUS pecking!' He pointed to his beak. 'You see this? This is a beak, this is, and unless you want to see it in action, close up, MOVE!'

The canaries looked anxiously at Horace.

What was he going to do? Nobody spoke to the canaries like that. The seagull was going to get his beak rammed down his throat if he wasn't careful. Horace stood up slowly and calmly. The canaries held their breath.

'All right,' he said, 'all right. We all make mistakes. We accidentally landed on your roosting place.'

The canaries gasped; they couldn't believe their ears. Horace gestured to them to be quiet.

'We don't want any trouble, mister. We'll go and find somewhere else to sleep.'

He turned to the dumbstruck canaries.

'You heard the gentleman – be so good as to follow me.'

So saying, he spread his wings and took off, his worried flock in formation behind him.

'What's the matter with him?' whispered Boris to Doris. 'I was ready to bash that seagull's beak in. He was asking for it!'

'It's not like Horace,' agreed Doris. 'Maybe it's the strain of the escape, gone to his head. Know what I mean?'

Horace led his flock of confused and muttering canaries higher and higher up into the sky. Far below, the seagull was still shouting and laughing.

'What's big and white and hates canaries? Me! I hate stupid little yellow birdies who are all beak and no bottle! Ha ha! What a laugh. . .!'

High up in the sky, Horace stopped and turned to his flock.

'I heard what you were saying earlier,' he said, 'and you're wrong. We are going back down to continue our conversation with that seagull. Assume attack formation!'

The canaries cheered.

'Thinks he can frighten a few little songbirds, does he?' growled Doris. 'I know a song we can sing to him. Come on, everybody!'

'Here we go, here we go, here we go!' chanted the canaries as they hurtled out of the sky towards the unsuspecting seagull.

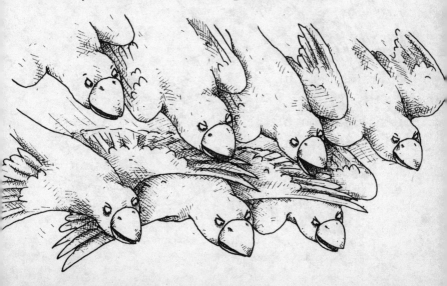

'Here we come, here we come, here we co-ome!'

The seagull was still boasting about his success.

'What's yellow and yellow?' he was shouting. 'Ha ha! That's a good one. What's yellow and *AAAAAAAGHKK*!!'

A tight formation of super-fit canaries whacked him clean off the top of the statue. With a gasp and a grunt, the seagull flapped raggedly to the ground.

'What's big and white and going to find somewhere else to sleep?' shouted Horace, zooming past the seagull's head as it limped off.

'What's small, yellow and unbeatable?' cried Norris.

'We are!' yelled the canaries as they settled down to sleep once more, this time confident of an uninterrupted night.

CHAPTER 7

YELLOW MISCHIEF

Some days later, in a quiet suburb, Timothy Crane, aged eight, was sitting in his Auntie Eileen's garden. On his lap was a plate with three rock cakes on it. He didn't like his Auntie Eileen's rock cakes. Nobody did. There was too much rock and not enough cake about them for his liking, but he knew that he would have to eat them. Little boys, as far as his Auntie Eileen was concerned, ate what they were given. It was good for them.

'Eat up your nice rock cakes, Timothy,' she called as she crossed the lawn towards him. He groaned inwardly. Suddenly there was a 'Whooosh!', a flash of yellow in the region of Timothy's plate, and no cakes.

'Good gracious!' cried Auntie Eileen. 'Your lovely rock cakes, gone! What on earth did that? Did you see?'

'No,' said Timothy.

'Those were the last ones!' wailed Auntie Eileen. 'How awful!'

'Awful,' echoed Timothy, trying not to look pleased.

The canaries' raids weren't always as welcome as this. Usually their victims weren't at all happy about their vanishing food. The canaries didn't care. They snatched sandwiches from people coming out of snack bars and bakers' shops. They swooped on picnickers and rifled their lunchboxes. Even fish and chip shops became targets. There would be a whoosh, a flash of yellow, and no chips. They stole whole loaves of bread from bakers' vans, carrying the loaves between them to the nearest rooftop where they would peck them into more manageable pieces.

It didn't stop there. They raided pet shops and made off with whole bags of deluxe canary seed. They zoomed through open french windows and swiped buns and cakes from people's tea tables.

They even managed to steal themselves a kind of uniform.

'Check this!' cried Doris, parading in front of a scrap of mirror they had found. 'The winner of the Stylish Songbird of the Year Award, by a majority verdict. Ms Super-cool, the queen of good taste!' She adjusted her beret to a more outrageous angle. 'What's yellow and so sharp it hurts to look at it? Me!'

Doris's outfit was the result of a daring raid on a toy shop. The canaries had swooped in at lightning speed and snatched a selection of doll-sized jackets, berets and dark glasses. They had pecked the sleeves off the jackets so that they could fly in them.

Boris was having trouble with his buttons.

'Isn't that a bit tight, Boris?' asked Morris.

'I think it makes me look slimmer,' said Boris. 'It's the new, leaner Boris.'

'Don't be daft, it's too small!' put in Clarice. 'You look like a burst sausage. Why don't you swap with Alice? She's walking around looking like a tent with legs.'

'I heard that!' cried Alice. 'I'm going for the loose-fitting look. I think it's very stylish – not that you'd understand.'

With their uniforms and dark glasses on, they looked a tough and sinister bunch. Pretty soon word got round that you didn't mess with these canaries if you knew what was good for you.

CHAPTER 8

FITNESS, NOT FATNESS

Horace looked at his flock as they dozed in the sun. They had just eaten a large doughnut. Telltale grains of sugar stuck to their feathers, and most of them had smears of jam around their beaks. Horace wasn't impressed. He frowned.

The canaries were doing well. They had plenty of food, they had shelter, and nobody tried to make them sing. Life was easy. Horace felt it was too easy.

'We're losing our edge,' he complained, brushing sugar off his own feathers. 'We're not fit – we're fat and lazy. Look at us!'

'Oh, I don't know,' said Boris, standing up and squinting down at his impressive bulk. 'I may have thickened up a little, but I wouldn't say I'm fat.'

'You've thickened up all right, Boris,' put in Doris. 'If you can't see that the round, soft thing sticking out from under your jacket is a fat stomach, man, you must be really thick! Know what I'm saying?'

'All right, all right!' retorted Boris. 'You're not exactly dainty Doris any more, are you? I can't see you bouncing nimbly from twig to twig the way you look now. The tree would fall down.'

'Come on, you lot,' said Horace. 'We all know we're too fat for our own good. We're going to start exercising again, starting tomorrow!'

The canaries groaned, but they knew Horace was right. He always was – that's why he was their leader.

True to his word, the next day Horace organized keep-fit sessions on a nearby flat roof, and the flock began getting back into shape. They puffed and groaned as they did their wing stretches and controlled beak twists, but Horace pretended not to hear as he led them through a vigorous routine designed to tone up every muscle in their bodies.

'It's for your own good!' he reminded them. The canaries groaned.

It was during one of these exercise sessions that Doris heard something strange coming from the big plane tree over the road. It was a voice. A harsh-sounding voice, but definitely a sad one.

'Who's a lost boy then?' it wailed. 'Who's a hungry boy? Poor Polly's all alone. Poor Polly, poor Polly.'

The voice went on like this, rising and falling. Whatever creature it was, it wasn't happy. Doris squinted at the tree. There was a large greenish creature sitting huddled in one of the lower branches. Was it a bird? She called Horace over to have a look.

'It looks like some kind of bird,' said Horace finally. 'It also looks like it needs help. I think we should go over and see if there's anything we can do.'

The large green bird was actually a parrot, but it was in such a state that it looked like a ball of dirty green feathers more than anything else. The canaries had never seen a parrot before, even on Ralph's television, but they could tell it was a bird by its beak and claws.

Horace flew down and landed on the branch above the parrot.

'Hello, are you all right?' he asked.

'I'm a poor, poor boy,' groaned the parrot. 'Lost and alone. Poor Polly!'

It didn't seem to notice that Horace was there.

'Are you OK?' asked Horace again, louder this time.

The parrot started.

'Who are you?' it quavered. 'What do you want?'

'We want to help you,' explained Horace. 'What's the matter? Where have you come from? Perhaps we can help you to get back home. We're friends.'

'Friends?' groaned the parrot. 'I haven't got any friends.'

'Yes, you have,' said Horace calmly. 'We are your friends – we'll help you. Are you hungry?'

The parrot nodded weakly.

'I haven't eaten for three days,' he admitted. 'Not since the day before I left my cage. Why, oh why, did I ever run away?' He clapped a dirty wingtip to his forehead, dislodging a cloud of dust.

'It's my own fault! The cage door was left open, and I couldn't resist it. I just hopped out. I'd always wanted to see the world, and now I had my chance. What a fool I was!' The parrot broke down in a fit of sobbing and wailing.

Horace decided that they could help the parrot better if they got him up to their flat roof.

This proved difficult as he was too weak to fly, but by getting him to hop up to the higher branches of the tree, they put him within reach of the telephone wire that ran up to their roof.

When the parrot got there, he collapsed in a heap. The canaries helped him to stand up, then they brushed him down as best they could with bits of twig and dead matches. The worst lumps of grit and old chewing gum had to be pecked off.

When they had finished they gave him some leftover seed and an old cheese sandwich they had found earlier.

When he'd had enough, the parrot leaned back against the parapet and sighed.

'I don't know how to thank you,' he began. 'You've saved my life! I was in a bad way just now. I don't think I could have lasted another day without food.' He shook his head slowly.

'I suppose I'd better do some explaining. My name is Neville, but people call me Polly. They always call parrots Polly – I don't know why, but they do. Anyway, I'm a parrot and, until recently, I was living in the house of the

Lord Mayor.' The canaries whistled. This was obviously one high-up pampered parrot.

'I was kept in a great big cage. It was warm, cosy, clean and very, very grand. I had all the food I could eat. The Lord Mayor absolutely adored me, of course. He used to feed me bits of chocolate and special exotic nuts. Then he'd try and get me to say all sorts of things like, "Who's a pretty boy?"

'He also got me to say rude words, then he'd fall about laughing. Pretty childish, I thought, but I suppose it kept him amused. Well, one evening, after an hour or so of trying to teach me to say "Polly bites your bum!", which was not the sort of thing you'd expect from a Lord Mayor, he fell asleep in his armchair. He'd had one sherry too many, if you ask me. Anyway, he'd left the cage door open. Not only that – the window was open too! Well, what's a courageous parrot of character supposed to do?' He shrugged his wings and looked around at his audience.

I wish it had been that easy for us, thought Boris. What a stroke of luck!

'You can guess what I did,' continued Neville. 'I would never get a chance like that again, so I took it, hopped out and, well, here I am.'

Yes indeed, there he was – a large green parrot with obviously very little idea of how to look after himself. Now that the canaries had rescued him, they had a problem. What on earth were they going to do with him?

If the canaries had been more observant, they might have noticed a large white shape lurking in the shade of an ornate parapet on the far side of the square.

The seagull, for that's who it was, was still

smarting over his humiliating defeat and was spying on them from a safe distance. Ever since the argument at the statue he had had to share a window-ledge roost with two fat pigeons and a crow called Denis, who snored. He wanted revenge.

'I'll get those canaries,' he swore, grinding his beak in frustration. 'I don't know how, but I'll get them!'

CHAPTER 9

YELLOW, 'ELLO, 'ELLO

At police headquarters, Inspector Jones was sitting at his desk, catching up on some report writing, when there was a knock at his office door. It was Sergeant Cummings, his assistant.

'Come in, Cummings,' said Inspector Jones, chuckling to himself. 'Ha, ha! I love saying that.'

'I know you do, sir,' said Sergeant Cummings.

'All right, Cummings,' sighed the Inspector. 'You have to allow me my little joke from time to time. What is it you wanted?'

'It's time for the Canary Committee meeting in room twelve, sir,' said Cummings.

'So it is, so it is,' said Inspector Jones, getting up and straightening his jacket. 'What are we to do about them, eh? Those naughty little birdies.'

'Blow them out of the sky, sir,' said Cummings.

'Hmmm. . . A bit extreme perhaps,' mused Inspector Jones, 'blasting them to smithereens with anti-aircraft fire? Oh well, the committee shall decide, one hopes.'

The Canary Committee sat round a large table in room twelve. Inspector Jones walked in and sat down. Around him the committee members' faces were stern.

'Well, Jones?' enquired the Lord Mayor impatiently. 'Got any bright ideas? We need to do something about these canaries, and fast! It's not right them flouting the laws of the land. They're just taking what they want, when they want it!' He banged the table. 'I say we blast them out of the sky!'

'With respect, Your Worship,' said Inspector Jones, 'though I take your point, the laws of the land don't really apply to canaries. And anyway, if they did I doubt you could impose the death penalty for stealing food.'

The Lord Mayor snorted.

'All right,' he said reluctantly, 'no guns. But we can't let them get away with it. I've had letters.'

'So have I,' said Jones. 'But if we shoot them, we'll get a lot more letters, not to mention the national Press and television after us. We've got to catch them alive, with as little fuss as possible.'

'All right,' said the Mayor, 'point taken, but how are you going to do it?'

The Inspector outlined his plan.

'Hmmm,' said the Lord Mayor, 'it's not what you might call inspired, but it might work. I suppose we ought to give it a try.' He paused thoughtfully. 'Oh, and while you're here, Jones, any news of my parrot? He's been gone a week, and I'm fair heartbroken, I can tell you. But I'm getting some posters printed, offering a reward, so if you get any information you must let me know immediately.' He shook his head sadly. 'I don't know what I'll do if we don't find him before the Lord Mayor's parade next month.'

The Lord Mayor sighed heavily. He was fond of his parrot and missed him deeply.

The Inspector's less-than-inspired plan involved forming the canary squad, a group of men with nets, lights, a selection of sandwiches and a special van. The van was equipped with a new sort of radar which could pick out small flying objects like flocks of birds. It even had a 'Yellow Alert' button for when the canaries appeared on the radar screen. It was disguised as an ordinary, slightly tatty, white van.

The idea was basically to set a trap. The man with the sandwich would sit in a conspicuous place and pretend to eat it. The men with the lights would hide in the bushes behind him with the netsmen, who were poised to leap out at the crucial moment.

When the canaries made their sandwich swoop, the lights would dazzle them and the netsmen would jump out and catch them in their nets. This was the theory at any rate.

In order to position their trap in the most likely place, the police had to know where the canaries were. To help find this out they put up 'Wanted' posters all over town, offering a reward for information leading to the canaries' capture. Then they waited.

CHAPTER 10

WHAT'S GREEN AND A PAIN IN THE BEAK?

'Are you sure you don't want to go home?' asked Boris, pointedly. He addressed his remark to Neville the parrot, who was flying awkwardly amongst the otherwise ordered formation of canaries.

'Yeah, man, won't the old Lord Mayor be missing you?' added Doris, dropping a heavy hint.

'No, he'll be all right,' said Neville. 'I'll stay here with you lot.' He chuckled. 'Your lives won't be the same now you've got me here to give you a guiding hand!'

Horace didn't doubt it. He suppressed the urge to tell Neville that what he needed was a guiding hand round his throat. He ground his beak in annoyance, but stayed silent.

He had spotted a man eating a bag of crisps in the park below. Roast-beef flavour – his favourite. He nudged Boris.

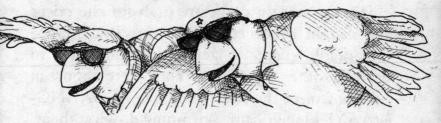

'Down there,' he whispered.

'Yeah,' said Boris. 'Nice one!'

At a signal from Horace, the canaries assumed attack formation and dived towards their target.

'Oh, right!' said Neville. 'We're going down there, are we? OK then, come on, everybody, we're going down there! Oh, they've gone. Oy! Wait for me!' He flapped down after them.

Horace and Boris were lining themselves up for the crisp grab, Norris and Doris in support, when there was a dreadful screeching noise. It was Neville, flapping down behind them, and he was picking up speed.

'WHEEEEEE!' he squawked. 'I'm catching you! YAHOOOO!'

The crisp-eater looked up, startled by the noise. Four canaries and a screaming parrot were converging on him at high speed.

'Wha. . .?' he spluttered, ducking instinctively.

Horace made a desperate grab for the crisps and caught a corner of the bag. Boris, by a remarkable piece of aerobatics, managed to grab the other top corner. They were almost in full control of the situation when, 'GAAANG-WAAY!' Neville came screaming down at them, out of control.

'You're doing it all wrong!' he was shouting. 'You should. . .'

They never found out what it was they should. . . There was a crash, a cloud of crisps, and Horace and Boris were knocked flying. Norris' dark glasses fell off, and Doris' beret was flung into a puddle.

Neville the parrot did a kind of out-of-control somersault in midair and landed in a wastepaper bin in a storm of crisp fragments. The other canaries took rapid evasive action.

'What a disaster!' cried Boris as the canaries

flew hurriedly away. 'What does that great green pillock think he's up to?'

'Look at my beret, man! Look at my beret!' Doris was livid. 'How can I be a cool canary with a beret that looks like something I found in a swamp!'

'He's got to go!' growled Norris. 'He's got to go!'

'Hey!' cried an all too familiar voice. 'Wait for me!' Neville flapped up level with them.

'I've got a bone to pick with you lot,' he announced. 'How am I supposed to help you if you get in my way all the time? It's not on you know.'

Norris choked, and Boris looked as though he might explode at any minute.

'You obviously need proper planning,' continued Neville. 'Then we won't get everybody trying to do the same thing all at once, will we?' He looked round and chuckled.

'Oh well, no harm done. All I can say is, it was your lucky day when you bumped into me, because planning is my game. Just call me Polly the planner!'

'How about Polly the dead planner?' said Boris, under his breath. 'How are we going to get rid of this ridiculous bird?'

CHAPTER 11

WHAT'S YELLOW AND WANTED?

The canaries flew on in angry silence, Neville flapping erratically behind them. As they passed the old, disused cinema by the park, something caught Horace's eye. Amongst the posters advertising various musical events was one which said 'Have you seen these birds?' in big letters above a picture of a bunch of what were supposed to be canaries, in dark glasses and berets.

'What the. . .?' spluttered Horace, swerving violently.

It was a 'Wanted' poster about the canaries, offering a reward for information leading to their capture. The picture itself was an artist's impression as there were no photographs of the canaries available, or for that matter in existence. It wasn't a very good artist's impression.

Horace was disgusted.

'What a load of rubbish!' he exclaimed. 'That doesn't look anything like us. Not one

WANTED

HAVE YOU SEEN THESE BIRDS?

RING 081-727-006X

bit. That's just a picture of a bunch of non-descript birds with pathetic hats on.' He flapped his wings in irritation. 'If they must put a price on our heads, they could at least draw them properly!'

'Is that supposed to be me?' cried Doris, aghast, looking at one of the canaries on the poster. 'That's too much, man. I mean, that is seriously out of order.' She grabbed Boris's wing. 'Look at that! Can you honestly say that excuse for a canary looks like me?'

'Better looking if anything,' said Boris. 'Wait a minute, is that big, misshapen lump in the background supposed to be me?'

'An understatement of the truth,' said Doris, getting her own back.

'This poster is an insult!' cried Alice.

'Why couldn't they have got someone who could draw?' complained Clarice. 'Or at least tried to get a photograph!'

Horace was deeply upset. He was annoyed about the poster, but he was more concerned about the fact that the authorities were out to get them.

He perched on a bollard and thought for a while in moody silence, until his reverie was interrupted by an anguished wail from Neville.

'Look at this!' he cried. The canaries gathered round. He was looking at another poster. This one had a picture of a large green parrot on it, and the word 'REWARD' in big letters across the top. 'They're after me, too!' he wailed.

CHAPTER 12

WHAT'S DRESSED IN BLUE AND PRETTY PATHETIC?

Despite the poster campaign, the specially formed canary squad was not a success. The radar was inaccurate and kept giving false alarms. Canary Control received scores of calls, but they gave conflicting information, so the canary squad never knew for sure where the canaries actually were. And anyway, by the time they got there the canaries were long gone, if indeed they had been there at all.

It was a disaster. They decided to change their tactics and, instead of trying to find the canaries, would stay in the most likely spot and hope that the canaries would find them. Needless to say, morale in the canary squad was not high.

Inspector Jones' assistant, Sergeant Cummings, had made sure that when the canary squad was formed, he was in it. He had wanted the canaries to be blown out of the sky, but when that idea was overruled he wanted at least to play a part in their capture. The fact that the canary squad was plainly unsuccessful angered him.

'Those canaries are making us look stupid!' he exclaimed to his colleagues. 'If I had my shotgun. . . ' He left the sentence unfinished.

Outside the van, the seagull was hanging around, listening. He had noticed a group of policemen with what looked like nets and lights, getting into a van. There had been rumours about a canary snatch squad from the sparrows that nested on the police station roof, and he had kept his eyes open. If the canaries were going to be caught, he wanted to witness it.

It seemed that he had guessed right – this was indeed some kind of canary-trapping operation. He decided to stay within earshot and see what information he could pick up. Perhaps there would be some way he could help the police.

In the van, Sergeant Cummings was still complaining.

'Do you remember that great big hawk we used to use to stop the pigeons roosting on the Town Hall?'

'I remember,' exclaimed one of his colleagues. 'He was a nasty piece of work, he was. You were his handler, weren't you?'

'That's right, I was his handler,' said Cummings, 'but he was all right with me. We had an understanding, you might say. He seemed to like me. At least, he used to do what I told him most of the time. Anyway, if we had him around today we could sort those canaries out good and proper, instead of all this sitting around with stupid sandwiches.'

The seagull was listening with interest. A hawk? What a good idea.

'What happened to him?' asked Cummings' colleague.

'They stopped using him. Said it was too expensive keeping a hawk just to scare pigeons. Anyway, he'd been getting a bit weird towards the end – started wearing an eyepatch and gold rings on his legs. I let him go. He lives in an old church tower out west of here now. Calls himself Nasty Nasty or somesuch. Completely off his head, of course. It's sad really.'

The seagull was exultant. He jumped up and down and punched the air with his wing. Now he knew how to get his revenge on those cocky little canaries! Nasty Nasty would tear them into little pieces, which was no more than they deserved. Now to find that old church tower.

CHAPTER 13

POLLY THE PLANNER HAS A PLAUSIBLE PLAN

Ever since the canaries had got back to their flat roof, Horace hadn't uttered a word. He sat apart from the others, lost in thought. Neville was uncharacteristically quiet too. He seemed to be going over and over something in his mind, trying to make a difficult decision. The sight of the 'Wanted' poster had obviously shaken him up. Eventually he hopped over to Horace's perch.

'Ahem!' he coughed.

Horace looked at him without much interest. 'Yes?' he said, testily. 'Did you want something?'

'Well, actually, I've been thinking,' began Neville. Horace fought back the desire to say something sarcastic like, 'That makes a change.'

'It's about those posters,' Neville continued. 'I'm very worried about them. This could be more serious than you think. Serious for you, I mean.' Neville shuffled his feet nervously.

'You see, if we're seen together and someone tells the police, they're going to think that I've been kidnapped by those wicked canaries, which would mean even more trouble for you if you're caught. They won't believe that I'm with you of my own free will.'

'Go on,' said Horace.

'Have you ever heard of the R.C.C.V.C.B.?'

'No,' said Horace. 'What on earth's the R.C . . . whatever you said?'

'The Rehabilitation Centre for Criminally Violent Caged Birds,' continued Neville. 'It's where they send birds they think are antisocial or dangerous. I met a budgie once who'd been there. It's a terrible place, he said. I couldn't live with myself if you got sent there on my account.'

'You really think they'd send us there?' said Horace.

'I do,' said Neville. 'The Lord Mayor would insist on it if he thought you'd kidnapped me.'

'This is serious,' said Horace, 'and it's going to need some thought.'

'Well, I've been working something out,' said Neville. 'It's important to get the Lord Mayor on your side and, with my help, I think you can do it.'

CHAPTER 14
THE PATHS OF NASTINESS

The seagull flapped uncertainly towards the old, ruined church tower. He noticed several bats flying in and out of the holes in the stonework, and shuddered. He didn't like bats; it made his feathers itch just thinking about them, horrible things. But this was where Nasty Nasty was to be found, and it was Nasty Nasty he wanted to see.

He flapped through a gaping hole in the old belfry wall and perched on a beam.

He didn't have to wait long. Almost immediately, with a mysterious hissing and twittering sound, five starlings, all wearing eye patches, appeared next to him.

'Can I help you?' one hissed in a menacing voice, peering at the seagull through his unpatched eye. 'Do you wish to see someone or have you accidentally strayed into the paths of Nastiness?'

The starlings all laughed in an unpleasant way. These were no ordinary birds; they were the Sinister Starlings, servants and bodyguards to His Nastiness, Nasty Nasty himself.

'I want to see the boss,' said the seagull.

'Of course you do,' sneered the starling. 'But does the boss want to see you?'

'Who wants to see the boss?' said a harsh, whining voice. 'Someone interesting? I think not – just a seagull and, not to put too fine a point on it, a rather common sort of seagull.'

A large black and white falcon flew down and landed on a special perch on the other side of the belfry. This was the boss, otherwise known as Nasty Nasty, ex-police hawk and one-time scourge of the Town Hall's pigeons. His appearance matched his name. Sergeant Cummings was right when he said the hawk had gone a bit weird since his departure from the force.

He wore a black eyepatch with the letters NN picked out in diamonds on the centre. His unpatched eye glinted nastily, as if trying to compensate for being the only one visible. His beak was curved like a scimitar and came to a thoroughly dangerous point. As he stretched his enormous wings, the gold rings on his legs rattled against one another, drawing the seagull's attention to his uncomfortably sharp talons. All in all, the hawk was an awesome sight.

'What does the common-looking seagull want, eh?' Nasty Nasty whined. 'It had better be something interesting.' He tilted his head to one side. 'As you might have gathered, I am the boss. Feel free to be awestruck, but don't forget to state your business.'

'You're Nasty Nasty?' asked the seagull, wanting to be sure.

'Ye-es,' said the falcon, patiently. 'Please state your business. My time is precious, unlike yours. I doubt if anything of yours is precious.'

'Well,' began the seagull, looking round furtively, 'my business is this. . . I've a message from Sergeant Cummings concerning a certain bunch of canaries. I get the impression that he'd prefer it if they weren't around. . .'

CHAPTER 15

WHAT'S GREEN AND GOING HOME?

'This looks like a good place,' said Boris, looking at a heap of dust, dirt and litter that had been left in a corner of the square. 'You're sure you want to go through with this?'

'It's a very necessary part of my plan,' said Neville, and he jumped into the middle of the pile of rubbish.

'Right!' he said, and proceeded to roll about in the dirt while the canaries threw bits of twig, leaves and cigarette ends at him.

When he was completely filthy, Neville reached round and tugged a couple of beakfuls of feathers out of his back.

'Ow!' he exclaimed. 'This had better be convincing enough.'

'You look perfect,' said Horace. 'Anyone would think you've been living in a gutter for the past month.'

'All right,' said Neville, 'let's go,' and he flapped off to a small tree not far from the Lord Mayor's house, but out of sight from it. The canaries followed.

'Now, you're really sure that this is what you want to do?' asked Horace. 'This is your last chance to back down.'

Neville grinned. 'I've made up my mind,' he said. 'I'm happy to give myself up if I know it's helping you. I haven't forgotten that you saved my life.'

The canaries muttered and looked at the ground in embarrassment.

'To be honest,' continued Neville, 'freedom was turning out tougher than I had ever expected. I couldn't survive on my own and I couldn't live off you for ever – it wouldn't be fair. No, the best place for me is my nice warm cage. Don't worry, I'll be all right. Come on, let's get it over with!'

The Lord Mayor was staring sadly out of his study window. The empty parrot cage, exactly as Neville had left it, stood on the table next to him. He watched idly as a group of sparrows fought over a crust of bread in the square below. Then something caught his eye – a flash of yellow and a glimpse of beret. He gasped. It was those blasted canaries!

He was in the act of reaching for the phone, when he stopped. There was something green with the canaries; something woefully tatty and dirty that limped along, supported on either side by a canary. It was Neville, his beloved parrot! With a stifled cry he flung open the window and leaned out. The group had reached his front steps by now. One of the canaries flew up and rang the doorbell.

The Lord Mayor leaped down the stairs three

at a time, which at his age was pretty good going, and flung the door open. There was his Neville, exhausted and starving (as far as the Lord Mayor knew, that is), lying gasping on his doorstep. Those canaries had obviously found him and brought him home. What fine, noble-hearted creatures they were! He had gravely misjudged them. He looked round, but suddenly the canaries were nowhere to be seen, so he scooped Neville up into his arms and bore him indoors.

CHAPTER 16
THE PEANUT PLOT

A group of small but sinister shapes slipped away from the old, ruined church tower, and flew purposefully towards the town. They carried something between them – a kind of package. No, not a package – a bag. A bag of peanuts.

'Fly, fly my darlings!' said a voice from the gloom of the tower. 'Fly to the appointed place. I shall join you there soon. When I arrive, the canaries shall suffer! Such a shame, inflicting nastiness on sweet little birdies, but such fun!' Nasty Nasty laughed. As he did so, his gold rings rattled gently.

The Sinister Starlings laid the bag of peanuts in a conspicuous place, and hid in a bush a short distance away, ready to jump out if necessary. They didn't want pigeons or squirrels ruining their plan. These were no ordinary peanuts. They were filled with explosive and were set to go off exactly twenty seconds after the bag was lifted off the ground.

'All set, my lovelies?' said Nasty Nasty as he swooped down into the bush. 'A ringside seat – marvellous. Let's hope our little yellow friends are hungry today.'

The lookout starling whistled.

'They approach, Your Nastiness,' he whispered.

'What fun!' sniggered Nasty Nasty to himself.

Doris and Alice were flying slightly ahead of the rest of the flock as the canaries made their way back to their flat roof. They noticed an unattended bag of peanuts lying on the ground near some bushes in the square below. They were hungry after escorting Neville back to the Lord Mayor's house, so they flew down to investigate.

'Peanuts, man,' said Doris. 'Unroasted, in their shells, with no added salt. Sounds seriously healthy to me. Let's see what the others think.'

'All right,' agreed Alice. 'Grab the other corner.'

In his hiding place, Nasty Nasty laughed softly to himself. 'Twenty seconds from now, and BANG! No canaries,' he giggled.

'One – two – three —' counted the Sinister Starlings as the two canaries took the bag up into the sky.

'Four – five – six —'

'Hey, everybody. We've found some un-roasted-still-in-their-shells-no-added-salt peanuts!' cried Doris.

'No additives, no "E" numbers,' added Alice, reading the packet.

'Ten – eleven – twelve —' counted the Sinister Starlings.

'Well, Boris has just spotted someone with a whole box of rum truffles,' said Horace. 'I'm sorry to disappoint you health freaks, but I know what I fancy and it's got more "E" numbers than you've had sunflower seeds.'

'A whole box, man?' Doris was outraged. 'You mean there's someone out there about to eat a whole box of rum truffles on their own? What a pig! Let's get in there.'

'No contest!' cried Alice. 'Let's give these nuts to the squirrels. Come on, drop them in those bushes there.'

Doris and Alice released their grip on the bag of peanuts and zoomed off after the others, in hot pursuit of rum truffles.

'Sixteen – seventeen – eighteen —' counted the Sinister Starlings, their eyes tightly shut and their wings over their ears in anticipation.

'Stand by for the yellow, feathery firework display!' gloated Nasty Nasty, shielding his eyes.

'Nineteen —' counted the starlings as something fell out of the sky into their bush. That something was the bag of peanuts. . .

'What was that bang?' asked Morris, startled.

'Probably terrorists,' said Clarice.

'Rubbish!' exclaimed Boris. 'It was a car backfiring. It happens all the time. Anyway, whatever it was, this is far more important. Look! The rum truffle man's dropped some! Quick, before the pigeons get them! Attack, attack, attack!'

The canaries zoomed down to relieve the man of his troublesome chocolates. They didn't notice the gently smoking remains of a bush below.

★

When the canaries got back to their flat roof, Horace was still in a thoughtful mood. They had all wanted to get rid of Neville, but now that he had gone, a kind of depression gripped them.

Horace mulled over what the parrot had said about the Rehabilitation Centre for Criminally Violent Caged Birds. This made him angry.

'How dare they put a price on our heads?' he growled. 'What harm have we done to them? Criminally violent? Ridiculous! It's not as if they can't spare the odd bit of food now and then. They throw away more food in a single day than we could eat in a year. Huh! These people need a reminder of just who they are dealing with!'

He hopped up on to the railings.

'Canaries!' he announced. 'There are those out there who wish to see us caged again! But we're not afraid of them. Canaries! We're going to shove their so-called artist's impression back in their faces!'

The canaries leapt up and cheered. They had no idea what Horace meant to do, but whatever it was, they were right behind him.

CHAPTER 17
SAY 'CHEESE'

Outside the railway station, next to a telephone box, was a passport photograph machine. Nearby, seven canaries in berets and dark glasses lurked in the shadows under the roof, watching carefully what went on.

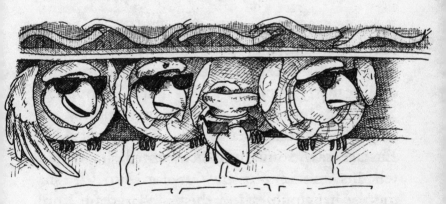

'They put four of those flat, round things in that hole and then go inside the box,' whispered Morris.

'Then some lights flash and they come out and stand around looking anxious for ten minutes,' observed Clarice, peering closely at the machine.

'Finally, the photographs appear in that slot there,' said Horace. 'How are we going to get hold of some of those round things?'

'I sometimes see them lying on the pavement,' put in Boris. 'Maybe we could scout around. With our sharp eyes we should be able to pick some up.

'Hmmm. . .' said Horace, thoughtfully, looking in the direction of the escalator. 'That might not be necessary.'

Eustace Crimble, aged six and three-quarters, was accompanying his mother out of the railway station. They had just been up to town to do some shopping. He liked shopping. Shopping meant people spending money on Eustace Crimble, even if they didn't want to. If Eustace saw something he wanted, he would tell his mother to buy it for him. If she didn't, he would stand there and scream until she did.

Eustace's mum, a harassed-looking woman in a brown coat, was stumbling along under the weight of several large parcels, all containing toys for Eustace. Toys that Eustace had screamed for.

'Come along, Eustace, darling,' she called. 'Come away from that dirty machine.'

Eustace had wandered up to the photo booth and stood looking at it with interest.

'I want my photograph taken,' he said, slowly and distinctly.

'Darling,' sighed his mother. 'You don't want to go into that awful, smelly machine. Daddy can take your photo when we get home.'

But Eustace *did* want to go into the awful, smelly machine and have his photo taken. He didn't want it taken when he got home, he wanted it taken in that machine, NOW! He opened his mouth and took a deep breath.

'All right, sweetie!' cried his mother, who knew the signs of an impending scream. 'All right. Here's some money. Just don't be long, that's all. I shall find us a taxi.'

Eustace took the money and advanced towards the machine.

In the shadows, Horace was watching carefully.

'This could be the opportunity we've been looking for!' he whispered to Morris. 'Tell the others to prepare for action when I give the word.'

'What a little monster!' whispered Alice. 'Doesn't he make your beak itch?'

'They're all monsters at that age,' whispered Clarice. 'It's a stage humans go through.'

'Yeah, they start off as little monsters and end up as great big monsters,' put in Boris.

'Shhh!' shushed Horace. 'Get ready.'

Eustace pushed past the small curtain, put the coins in the slot, then sat down on the stool. He put on his best smile; the one that his grandmas and aunties all said was so sweet, and which made them give him chocolates. Eustace liked chocolates. He made a mental note to do a scream outside a sweet shop on the way home. His smile grew wider at the thought.

Suddenly, something strange happened; something unusual and unpleasant. It started with a 'Whooosh!' Then something yellow flashed before his eyes. He felt a sharp pain in his nose.

'OWW!' shrieked Eustace.

FLASH! went the camera. He felt several sharp pains in the region of his bottom. FLASH! went the camera again.

'OWWOOO!' cried Eustace, jumping off the stool and stumbling out of the cubicle.

'WAAAH! Get them off me! WAAAH!' he wailed. He was so astonished that he forgot to scream. Then he remembered. He drew in a deep breath, and screamed.

Inside the cubicle, the canaries posed hurriedly. They had two shots left. FLASH! went the camera. They changed pose. FLASH! it went again.

'Quick, everybody, we'd better get out of sight!' cried Horace as the scream started outside.

They zoomed out of the photo machine and hid in the rafters. As far as they could tell, nobody had noticed them. The scream had stopped, but only for a moment. Eustace drew another huge breath and the onslaught continued. People were running from all over the place towards the noise. Eustace's mother was first on the scene, parcels falling left and right.

'Eustace! Sweetie pie! Darling! Are you all right?' she gasped. A policeman arrived and tried breathlessly to get some sense out of Eustace.

'All right, sonny,' he panted. 'What's been going on?'

'Oh, Officer,' cried his mother, above the

terrible noise. 'I think there's something dreadful in that photo booth. I let him go in because he wanted his photo taken. I turned my back for two minutes and he came running out, yelling his head off!'

The policeman went to look. He crept carefully up to the machine and whisked the curtain back. It was empty.

'There's nothing there now,' he said, bending down to address Eustace. 'What happened, sonny? Did you have a fright?'

Eustace nodded but didn't stop screaming. The policeman stood up, shaking his head.

'Well, I can't get any sense out of him,' he said to Eustace's mother. 'I suggest you take him home and put him to bed with a warm drink, and maybe call the doctor if he doesn't improve.' The policeman wanted to increase the distance between himself and Eustace's scream as quickly as possible.

Eustace allowed his mother to bundle him, still wailing, into a waiting taxi. The policeman dispersed the small crowd that had gathered, radioed his report to headquarters, then went on his way. Peace once more reigned by the photo machine.

Once the coast was clear, Horace cautiously stuck his head out from the canaries' hiding place in the rafters. The ten minutes must be very nearly up. Sure enough, the photo machine whirred and clanked a couple of times and a strip of paper with four photographs on it appeared in the slot provided.

Horace flew down, grabbed the still wet, chemical-smelling piece of paper and, signalling to his flock to follow him, zoomed off in the direction of the flat roof.

CHAPTER 18
NASTINESS UNSTUCK

Meanwhile, in the old, ruined church tower, a group of bedraggled starlings were fussing round a large falcon who was covered in what appeared to be fragments of peanut shell and bits of twig. He was missing several feathers.

'Come on you bunch of halfwits. Hurry up and get this distasteful muck off my feathers! If my eyepatch is damaged, I'm going to mangle those canaries!'

Nasty Nasty was living up to his name. The starlings had survived the explosion, but were definitely the worse for wear. They were dotted with bits of sticking plaster, and two of them had bandages on. They didn't look so sinister now as they tried to restore His Nastiness to his original condition.

'Those canaries!' swore Nasty Nasty. 'They are going to suffer for this. Nobody does this to me. I didn't get where I am today by being bombed by songbirds! Those little yellow unmentionables will be severely punished – *severely* punished.'

As the canaries came in to land on their flat roof with the photographs, feathery figures were watching from a nearby telegraph pole.

'All right, my feathered ones,' said Nasty Nasty. 'This time it's their turn to suffer and suffer they shall! What's yellow and not going to be around for much longer? Ha ha! Well, I know the answer to that question. If you don't, I'll give you a clue. It begins with "C" and they're over there.'

The Sinister Starlings laughed in their hissy, twittery way.

'You know what to do, my beauties. So do it!' cried Nasty Nasty.

There was an overhead electric cable attached to the same telegraph pole as the wire that ran up to the canaries' flat roof. The plan was to join them together, so that when the canaries settled on the wire, which they often did, they would be electrocuted. It was a thoroughly nasty plan.

The starlings were fussing and flapping around the dozen or so cables and wires attached to the telegraph pole. The wire had been attached to the power cable and was now very live and very dangerous. The starling holding it in its beak by its plastic coating was nervously trying to work out which of the many telephone wires it should be attached to.

Nasty Nasty was watching from his perch on the wire that ran to the next telegraph pole. He saw the starling hesitating.

'What's the idiot up to?' he said to himself. 'What's he doing? He's not. . . He is! The cretinous bird! That's the one I'm sitting on! No, you fool. Not that one!' he screamed. 'NO! NOT THAT ONE!'

CHAPTER 19
MUGSHOTS

The canaries gathered excitedly around the photographs. Everyone agreed they were brilliant! The one of Eustace's face while his bottom was being pecked was the best thing they'd seen in ages. They fell about laughing.

Horace seemed more interested in the last picture, which was a group shot. They stared out of the photograph, a tough bunch of superfit canaries. It was just what Horace had wanted.

'This is the one. Look at that!' he exclaimed and pecked along the join between the picture and the next one on the strip, tearing off the one he wanted.

'Sorry to interrupt,' said Morris, 'but I just heard a kind of strangled squawk – and there's a burning smell, a bit like frazzled feathers or something.'

'I wouldn't worry about it, Morris, me old mate,' said Boris. 'Come and look at this picture.' He pointed to himself. 'Now is that or is that not a fine figure of a canary?'

'Well, I look pretty good though I say it myself,' replied Morris, the squawk and the smell forgotten.

Horace was pleased.

'They want people to know what we look like, do they?' he cried, brandishing the photograph. 'Well, so do I. Come on, canaries! To the newspaper offices!'

Daily Cable reporter, Howard Byng, sat in his

office on the fourth floor of Big Newspapers House, with his feet on his desk. He was bored that afternoon. There was very little news, and consequently not much work to do.

He toyed with a paperclip, fiddled with his biro, and tried making interesting things with elastic bands and bits of screwed-up paper. It didn't help much. He was still bored. The interesting things he made kept falling apart, and anyway they weren't actually that interesting in the first place. He yawned and, as he did so, he caught something out of the corner of his eye. Something yellow. It was moving quite fast – very fast, in fact – and it was coming straight for him. Was it a bird? Was it a plane? No, it was definitely a bird and it had something in its beak. If it wasn't careful it was going to. . .

CRASH!

The bird smashed through the window as if it wasn't there, dropped a small piece of coloured paper on to Howard Byng's desk and zoomed out the way it came in. He noticed with astonishment that it was wearing a beret and dark glasses. He looked at the piece of paper and reached for the phone.

'Chief,' he said. 'I think there's something you should see!'

CHAPTER 20

F.U.N. TIME

The old, ruined church tower was the scene of much more activity than usual. Small groups of unpleasant-looking birds were arriving every few minutes, and the belfry rang, if that's the right word, with chirps, squawks and cackles of all kinds.

Nasty Nasty was standing in the centre of this hubbub, supported on either side by a Sinister Starling. His feet were bandaged so it was quite hard for him to grip his perch. He had managed to survive being electrocuted, but his feet and a couple of tail feathers had been burnt. He flapped his wings and the belfry fell silent.

'My unpleasant friends!' he began. 'I called this emergency F.U.N. (the Fellowship of Untold Nastiness) meeting because there is a job to be done. Don't let the word "job" put you off. It's not going to be difficult or tiresome. On the contrary. You won't have enjoyed yourselves so much for years! All you have to do is tear a few meddlesome canaries into little pieces!'

The birds in the belfry cheered and clicked their beaks, the seagull amongst them. This was their kind of job.

'Are you ready to fly with me, my nasties? Are you ready to seek out and destroy these yellow pests? Are you ready to avenge His Nastiness, Nasty Nasty, and restore his bad name?' He spread his wings wide.

The Fellowship of Untold Nastiness shrieked their agreement and followed Nasty Nasty in a great flock out of the belfry.

CHAPTER 21

WHAT'S YELLOW AND BIG NEWS?

The next day it was all over the front page of the *Daily Cable*.

'Yellow Peril? Songbirds in Surprise Sandwich Snatch Shocker,' screamed the front page headline. Underneath, the canaries' photograph had pride of place. The inside pages had smaller headlines, like: 'What's Yellow, Feathery and Filches Food?' There were eye-witness accounts of food raids, chip grabs and sandwich snatches from all over town.

There was even a picture of Brian Burton, of 'Burton's Lunchtime Bites', wielding a shotgun, saying that the canaries were a menace to society and should be shot.

To counter that, there was an article by someone from the R.S.P.B. about how some birds reacted badly to being caged.

'After all, how would you like it?' the R.S.P.B. man argued, and he went on to say that he admired the canaries' spirit. They were welcome to come and steal his sandwiches any time!

The paper sold in huge quantities and the canaries were even mentioned on national radio. It looked as if people were all set to go canary mad!

When they went on their morning patrol, the canaries noticed unusual things going on below them. People would stop, look up at them and point. They would peer at the canaries through binoculars. Sometimes people would cheer; other times they would throw things at them. Some people even held out sandwiches and bits of cake, as if inviting them to come and take them. It was very odd. Horace guided his flock high into the sky, out of the range of binoculars.

'How are we supposed to get anything to eat with all those people watching us?' complained Norris.

'How can we surprise them if they know where we are all the time? What's the matter with them?' cried Boris.

'It's those posters. I had a horrible feeling when I saw them,' said Clarice. 'We're all going to starve. I knew it would happen!'

'I get a horrible feeling every time you open your mouth,' said Morris. 'Clarice the optimist!'

'They're not looking at you lot anyway, man,' boasted Doris. 'The binoculars are fixed on me, and the people are saying "Who is that cool canary? Shame about the other scruffy songbirds she hangs around with." Don't you lot understand? We're famous!'

'All right, we're famous,' said Horace, 'which might be inconvenient for now, but it's not all bad. If we get caught – heaven forbid – it won't just be the police who decide what happens to us. They'll have public opinion to contend with. If we're celebrities it'll be hard for them to lock us away in some glorified prison for birds. Do you see what I'm getting at?'

Boris wrestled with the idea and then looked at Horace in awe.

'So that's why you took the photo to the newspaper!' he cried. 'To make us famous for our own protection! Phew! No wonder you were so quiet. It would have taken me a month to work that one out. I'm impressed!'

Doris and the others were dumbstruck once they had worked out what Horace was getting at. They stared, open-mouthed.

'Well, famous or not, we're going to have to use different tactics to get our food. It won't be easy but we must try and keep out of sight until the last minute. This excitement won't last – you know what humans are like. It'll quieten down in a few days.'

CHAPTER 22

LARGE AS LIFE AND TWICE AS YELLOW

The canaries flew back down to roof level in a quiet part of town, careful not to be seen. They patrolled by keeping to the rooftops, darting from building to building. Their food scouting was done by peering over gutters and round chimneys at the streets and squares below.

After an hour or two of this, all they had managed to find was an unattended sausage roll and an old cheese sandwich. That was pretty uninspiring fare compared to what they were used to. They hadn't been seen by anybody, but they weren't happy. Then Horace made a discovery.

'Well, well,' he muttered, peering over a gutter into the small square below. 'A policeman eating a sandwich! Looks like cheese and tomato on granary bread to me – a well-known canary favourite. I hope it's got pickle on it. I love pickle. This is too good to miss. Come on, canaries. Breakfast ahoy!'

'I'm so hungry I could eat a hundred sandwiches,' groaned Alice.

'Same here,' agreed Boris.

'Come on you lot,' said Horace. 'We'll eat the sandwich and Boris and Alice can eat the policeman. Let's go!'

Horace led the canaries high up into the sky above the sandwich-eating policeman.

In the canary squad van, which was parked a short distance away, the radar had picked up something. It was the type of reading made by a group of about seven small birds flying in formation. The radar operator immediately made radio contact.

'We have a minor Yellow Alert, boys,' he said. 'Assume action stations. Will keep you informed, OK?'

Then, on the edge of the screen, a larger blip appeared. This one was the type of reading made by a ragged flock of variously sized birds, and it was following the first blip.

Up in the sky, the Fellowship of Untold Nastiness had spotted the canaries.

'I can see them!' cried Nasty Nasty. 'There they are, large as life and twice as yellow! Attack, my massed nasties, attack!'

The canaries only had eyes for their target, the policeman's sandwich. They had no idea that they were a target themselves.

'This is high enough,' said Horace. 'Asssume attack formation. Let's go!'

The canaries dived steeply and began to pick up speed.

'They're trying to get away!' yelled Nasty Nasty. 'Come on, my fearless F.U.N.sters, dive, dive, DIVE!'

The radar screen now showed that the first, smaller formation was descending at speed towards the sandwich-wielding policeman.

'They've fallen for it, boys!' yelled the radar operator into his radio. 'This time it's for real. Yellow Alert! Yellow Alert!'

The radar screen showed that the second flock had also turned and was diving at speed after the first one.

The policeman holding the sandwich was beginning to look nervous. In the bushes, where the netsmen and lightsmen were hiding, the tension was mounting. Sergeant Cummings gripped his net tightly and squinted up into the sky.

CHAPTER 23

WHAT'S YELLOW AND IN CUSTODY?

The canaries zoomed towards their would-be breakfast, intent on one thing – the sandwich. They were hungry. They didn't see the partly concealed figures in the bushes behind, or the bits of net and cable sticking out here and there. They also didn't see the forces of Nastiness massed behind them and gaining all the time.

Suddenly, when they were only about twenty metres away from their target, a blinding light shone straight into their eyes. Despite their dark glasses, they were well and truly dazzled; they couldn't see a thing.

Nasty Nasty and the Fellowship of Untold Nastiness were travelling at quite a speed by now. Slowly but surely they were catching up with the canaries, who seemed totally oblivious of their presence.

'Those little yellow sandwich-stealers are due for a nasty surprise!' chuckled Nasty Nasty, flexing his talons in anticipation. But it was him that got the surprise when a blinding light struck his flock full in the eyes. With a chorus of screams and wails, the massed forces of Nastiness plummeted towards the square, out of control.

When the light hit him, Horace instinctively veered sharply to one side, and steered hard upwards to avoid hitting the ground. He hoped the others had done the same. As his eyes

recovered, he blinked at the hazy shapes around him. There was quite a commotion going on a short distance away. As his vision cleared, he began to make out what was happening.

Three jubilant policemen were carrying a net between them, and in the net were six yellow things – things that flapped uselessly against the netting. Horace's blood froze as the realization hit him that it had all been a trap! The policeman, the sandwich, everything! And he'd fallen for it lock, stock and barrel! What a fool he'd been! By some miracle he had managed to escape, but his flock had been captured. It was too much to bear.

Sergeant Cummings pointed to the canaries and winked at his colleagues.

'Anything you canaries say will be taken down and used in evidence against you!' he chuckled.

'Hey, Sarge!' called his colleague. 'How do you spell "Tweet, Tweet"?' The policemen guffawed loudly and climbed into the back of the canary squad van.

Horace was appalled. His flock! His friends! After all they had been through together, the thought of them being caged again was too much to bear.

'Don't worry!' he screamed. 'I'm coming! I'll save you!'

His scream coincided with a large splash as, behind him, the Fellowship of Untold Nastiness descended at speed straight into the fountain – Nasty Nasty, the seagull, Sinister Starlings, the lot.

Horace saw and heard none of this. His eyes blazing, he flew at full speed high up into the sky above the canary squad van, so high that it was just a dot. So high that only super-fit canary vision could pick out the van from its surroundings. Then he turned, adjusted his dark glasses and started to dive. The wind shrieked in his ears as he picked up speed.

'I'm coming for you, my brothers!' he screamed. 'Canaries for ever!'

Horace hit the back window of the van with a mighty crash, the glass broke, but no canaries flew out. They were in a super-strong cage inside. Horace was knocked unconscious.

CHAPTER 24

LONG LIVE THE LORD MAYOR!

In the courtroom, the atmosphere was tense. Although, technically, the canaries hadn't done anything against the law, they could be considered enough of a nuisance to the public to be permanently caged. This was what the police were pressing for. Their lawyer had made out a convincing case, and the canaries, excluding Horace, who was unconscious in hospital, anxiously watched the judge's face for signs of agreement. But the judge was giving nothing away.

Now it was the turn of the Defence. The canaries' lawyer stood up.

'My Lord, I call upon the Lord Mayor to speak for the canaries.'

There was much murmuring in the court. Inspector Jones looked dumbstruck. The last time he had seen the Lord Mayor, he was all for blowing the canaries out of the sky, and now here he was, speaking in their defence!

'Why's he speaking for us?' whispered Morris. 'We've never met him, have we?'

'It might be something to do with that parrot,' said Doris. 'He reckoned he could get the Lord Mayor on our side.'

'No twittering in court!' cried the judge.

There was a buzz of excitement as the Lord Mayor got to his feet.

'My Lord,' he began, 'as many of you will remember, a while ago the town's mascot, a large green parrot in my care, escaped. All searches for him were in vain. All hope had been lost and we were convinced that the parrot was gone for ever. The Lord Mayor's parade would have been a pale shadow of itself without the town's mascot, flapping bravely above the state coach in his regalia.' He shook his head gravely.

'All hope had been lost, that is, until these same canaries found that parrot and took pity on him. Knowing that he was too weak to fly, they fed him and walked him – yes, walked him; and I want you to think how dangerous it must be for a small songbird to walk any distance – walked him lovingly to my door. Waiting for no thanks, they flew off, completely unaware that I had witnessed the whole thing from my study window.'

The canaries looked at each other.

'So that's why Neville covered himself in all that muck!' exclaimed Alice.

'Don't you ever listen, man?' said Doris. 'That was his plan. Horace explained it all. Anyway, he's off again!'

The Lord Mayor flung his arms out.

'I appeal to this court, that in view of their compassionate and public-spirited behaviour, these noble but misguided birds should be dealt with leniently.'

There was cheering and applause from the public gallery.

'Keep talking,' muttered Boris, 'keep talking. If he carries on like this we'll get a knighthood not a prison sentence.'

'Silence in court!' snapped the judge.

The Lord Mayor looked round the court-room.

'These canaries,' he continued, 'have shown remarkable discipline and ingenuity in the way they live their lives. But these good qualities have been channelled into the wrong activities. I feel strongly that they should be allowed to put their energy into serving the community instead of wasting it, locked away in the Rehabilitation Centre for Criminally Violent Caged Birds.'

'What did all that mean?' whispered Clarice.

'He meant that he doesn't like what we do, but he likes the way we do it,' said Norris.

People in the public gallery cheered and were silenced by the judge banging his gavel and crying, 'Order!'

'I'm beginning to like this guy,' whispered Doris. 'I couldn't have put it better myself, know what I mean?'

'Sssshhhh. . . ' said Boris.

'No shushing in court!' cried the judge. The Lord Mayor continued.

'In the light of their compassionate nature and impressive discipline and organization, I have a position in mind for them that will, I believe, suit all parties,' he announced.

'What?' said Clarice.

'He's going to give us a job,' translated Norris.

CHAPTER 25

WHAT'S COMPLICATED BUT TURNS OUT ALL RIGHT IN THE END?

Horace lay in his hospital bed, feeling groggy and confused. He had only regained consciousness some twenty minutes earlier. Through the haze he was sure that he could hear voices, familiar voices, and they were getting louder.

He had just worked out that he was in hospital when the canaries burst into the room, chattering excitedly. They all cheered and whistled when they saw that Horace was awake.

'Thank goodness you're all right!' said Alice. 'We were all really worried. The doctor said if you hadn't been so fit you might not have survived the impact.'

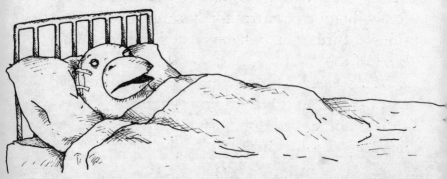

'Well, my head hurts and I'm a bit groggy, but apart from that I'm all right,' said Horace.

'You should see the back door of the van,' said Boris. 'That's in a bad way too.'

'Why aren't we all in prison?' asked Horace. 'And don't shout – I've got a bit of a headache.'

'Well,' said Clarice. 'We've got good news and bad news. Which do you want to hear first?'

'Give me the good news,' said Horace.

'All right,' said Doris. 'I'll tell you the good news as I'm the bright, cheerful type. Clarice can tell you the bad news.'

Clarice protested, but Doris went on.

'The good news is this. In view of how we rescued the Lord Mayor's parrot, and because the Lord Mayor thinks we're wonderful, noble canaries, they've given us a job instead of locking us up.'

'A job?' mused Horace. 'That's got to be better than sitting around in a cage in the Rehabilitation Centre for Criminally Violent Caged Birds, or whatever it's called. What kind of job?'

'Well,' said Doris, 'this is where the bad news comes in. Over to you, Clarice.'

'It's not a bad job,' said Clarice, 'but it's not a good job either.'

123

'Yes. . .?' prompted Horace. 'Just tell me what it is and put me out of my misery.'

'All right. It's Bodyguard to the Lord Mayor's parrot,' said Clarice.

'Bodyguard to the Lord Mayor's parrot?' echoed Horace. 'That's old Neville! That's not such a bad job. I'll have you know that if it wasn't for Neville's plan to get the Lord Mayor on our side, we'd be in the Rehabilitation Centre for Criminally Violent Caged Birds as I speak! He may be a pompous pain at times, but underneath he's all right.' The canaries looked suitably chastened.

'There's one thing that confuses me,' continued Horace. 'What does he need a bodyguard for?'

'The Lord Mayor's worried that he might escape again,' explained Norris.

'So we have to spend all day with Neville while he stuffs himself with exotic nuts and tells us how to run our lives,' grinned Horace. 'Oh well, it could be a lot worse.'

In the end, the job wasn't as bad as they thought it might be. The canaries' duties consisted of taking Neville for a daily exercise flight over the square, making sure he didn't try to escape again. Then they had to do a morning and evening patrol flight around the house to check that the windows were closed and the cage door shut correctly. The rest of the day was their own. They were well fed and were given a special uniform to wear which they all liked, even Doris. Life wasn't bad at all. Neville the parrot irritated them at times, but mostly he was a lot of fun, once he'd stopped trying to impress them all the time.

'Well,' said Boris, reaching for the last piece of the cream cake the Lord Mayor had given them. 'Six months ago, if anyone had told me that I'd end up eating cream cakes in the Lord Mayor's study, free to come and go as I please, more or less, I wouldn't have believed them. In fact I'd have thought that they were completely off their trolley as they say.'

The canaries murmured in agreement.

'Yeah, man.' said Doris. 'Unlikely is not the word! You'd have to be at least one bar short of a full cage to predict something like this, know what I mean?'

Horace laughed. 'Well, it turned out all right

in the end. I'm not one hundred per cent sure how, but it did. We should be thankful for that.'

'Thankful to me, you mean!' put in Neville, modest as always. 'If it wasn't for me you wouldn't be here.'

'Pah!' snorted Alice, 'What's green, with a big head and no brain? Neville! If it wasn't for us, YOU wouldn't be alive, let alone here!'

'All right, all right!' grinned Neville. 'We can be thankful to each other then.' He jumped up and prodded Boris playfully in the stomach. 'What's yellow and covered in cream?' he shouted, making a dash for the window. 'You lot! You look like the remains of a lemon meringue pie!'

The canaries jumped up and, with whoops and yodels, pursued Neville out of the window, round the square, in and out of the trees, and, finally, back into the Lord Mayor's study where they spent a happy five minutes throwing left-over bits of cream at each other. It was all great fun.

The cream cake and the chase made them feel pleasantly drowsy, and when the Lord Mayor looked into the room half an hour later he smiled as he saw a dishevelled, cream-spattered bunch

of canaries, and an equally dishevelled, cream-spattered parrot, fast asleep in a happy huddle with their backs against the radiator.

Life at the Lord Mayor's wasn't all riotous fun; there were ceremonial duties to carry out too. That was the part of the job Horace enjoyed most.

The canaries' task was to accompany the Lord Mayor and his official parrot, Neville, on state occasions. The Lord Mayor would ride in his gold coach, in his grand uniform, his parrot on his shoulder, also in a grand uniform, with his official bodyguards, the canaries, in *their* grand uniforms, flying in tight formation above him, proud and free.

Everybody who saw them said what a magnificent sight they were. Everybody except a tatty looking seagull, and a large, black and white falcon with an eyepatch and a limp, who glowered at them from the safety of a nearby tree.

'Those canaries haven't seen the last of us!' they growled unconvincingly.

THE END